Party Central

Adapted by Kristen L. Depken
Based on the original story by Kelsey Mann

A Random House PICTUREBACK® Book

Random House 🏠 New York

Copyright © 2014 Disney·Pixar. All rights reserved. Published in the United States by Random House Children's Books,
a division of Random House LLC, 1745 Broadway, New York, NY 10019, and in Canada by Random House of Canada Limited,
Toronto, Penguin Random House Companies, in conjunction with Disney Enterprises, Inc. Pictureback, Random House, and
the Random House colophon are registered trademarks of Random House LLC.
ISBN 978-0-7364-3179-8
randomhouse.com/kids
Printed in the United States of America
10 9 8 7 6 5 4 3 2 1

At Monsters University, all the fraternities and sororities were having huge parties . . .

. . . except for the **Oozma Kappas**.

"Face it, guys," said Terri and Terry. "No one's coming to our party."

Just then, Mike and Sulley burst through the front door.

"We thought this might happen," said Sulley, looking around the empty room.

"And that is why we came prepared!" added Mike.

Mike pulled a walkie-talkie out of a duffel bag and set something up in the **OK** living room. It was a door station that monsters used to enter the human world!

Meanwhile, Sulley set up another door station at the **Roar Omega Roar** fraternity house—where a huge party was in full swing.

"Beach Ball to Throw Rug, are you in position?" Mike said into his walkie-talkie.

"Roger that, Beach Ball," Sulley replied. "Operation Party Central is a go."

A few minutes later, Sulley stepped through the **ROR** door station with a cooler full of soft drinks he'd taken from the party. The door led into the bedroom of two human parents. Sulley tiptoed past the sleeping adults and through another door, which led . . .

. . . into the **Oozma Kappa** living room!

"We're not just going to throw the biggest party of the year," said Mike.

"We're going to steal it!" finished Sulley.

One by one, the **Oozma Kappas** lured partygoers
from the **ROR** side to the **OK** side.

"Welcome to Party Central!" Mike greeted them as Squishy opened a box of pizza.

"Well, hello!" Don greeted another group of monsters with a tray

"Welcome, ladies!" said Mike when the **PNK** monsters were pushed through the door station on a couch.

As the monsters continued to pass between the doors in the human bedroom, the mom heard a noise.

"Something just went into the closet," she said.

"There's nothing in our closet, dear," said the dad.

Soon, the **ROR** house was empty!

The entire party had moved to the **OK** house—and it was a blast!
The crowd cheered as Squishy jumped onto the coffee table

"This is the best party ever!" someone shouted. And it was, until . . .

. . . Squishy's mom showed up!
"What is going on here?" she cried.

It looked like the party was over.
"Are you boys door-jamming?" yelled Ms. Squibbles.
"What's door-jamming?" asked Squishy, confused.

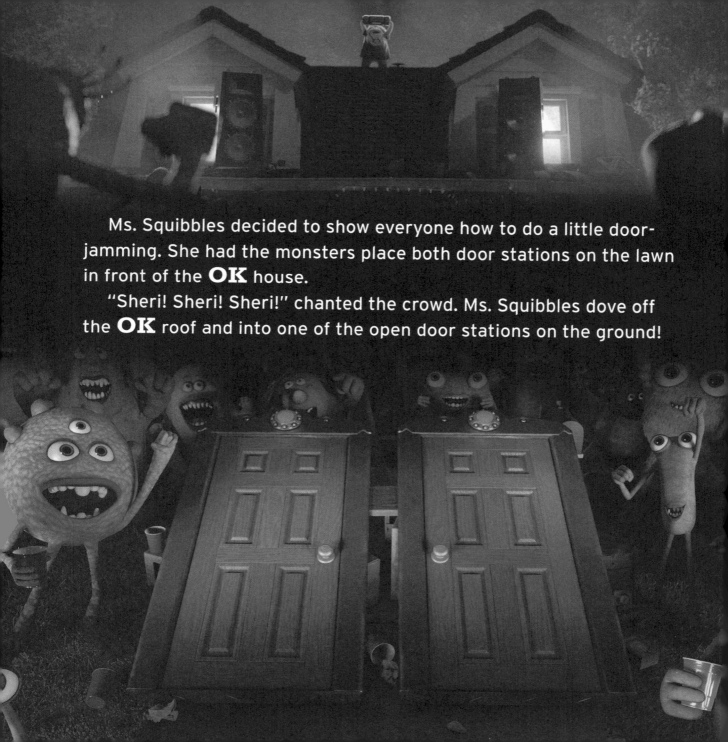

Ms. Squibbles decided to show everyone how to do a little door-jamming. She had the monsters place both door stations on the lawn in front of the **OK** house.

"Sheri! Sheri! Sheri!" chanted the crowd. Ms. Squibbles dove off the **OK** roof and into one of the open door stations on the ground!

In the human bedroom, the mom was sure there was something strange going on. She made the dad check their closet. He opened the door just in time to see . . .

. . . Squishy's mom diving right toward him!

She flew through the room and landed perfectly in the OKs' front yard.

Everyone cheered in amazement. The **Oozma Kappas** had thrown the best party MU had ever seen!